Dragon Slayers' Academy™ 6

SIR LANCELOT, WHERE ARE YOU?

By Kate McMullan

Illustrated by Bill Basso

GROSSET & DUNLAP • NEW YORK

For Ellecia Butchard
—K. McM.

visit us at www.abdopublishing.com

Published by Spotlight, a division of the ABDO Publishing Group, 8000
West 78th Street, Edina, Minnesota 55439. This library bound edition is
published by arrangement with Penguin Young Readers Group, a
member of Penguin Group (USA) Inc.

Library of Congress Cataloging-in-Publication Data
This title was previously cataloged with the following information:

McMullan, Kate.
    Sir Lancelot, where are you? / by Kate McMullan ; illustrated by Bill
Basso.
      p. cm. -- (Dragon Slayers' Academy ; 6)
    Summary: After the witch, Morgana le Fay, puts a curse on Sir
Lancelot, three knights-in-training from the Dragon Slayers' Academy
set out to save him.
    [1. Knights and knighthood--Fiction. 2. Trolls--Fiction. 3. Witches--
Fiction.] I. Basso, Bill, ill. II. Series: McMullan, Kate. Dragon Slayers'
Academy; 6.
PZ7.M47879S1 1999
[Fic]--dc21   99-20898

ISBN 978-1-59961-379-6 (Reinforced Library Bound Edition)

Chapter 1

We are off on a quest! Wiglaf thought happily. He stood with Angus and Erica at the foot of the Dragon Slayers' Academy drawbridge. *We shall save Sir Lancelot!*

A crowd of DSA students had come to see the three questers off. Wiglaf jiggled his pack impatiently. Would Headmaster Mordred *never* finish his good-bye speech?

Mordred stood on the drawbridge. "If Sir Lancelot offers you a reward for saving him, take it!" he told the questers. "But remember—any reward must be handed over to *me*! Uh... I mean, becomes the property of DSA."

Wiglaf worried as he listened. How would they save Sir Lancelot? The knight's evil twin brother, Leon, had paid the witch, Morgana le Fay, to put a curse on Lancelot. Wiglaf did not know what sort of curse it was. He knew only that Sir Lancelot had last been seen somewhere north of Camelot.

With Lancelot out of the way, Leon had pretended to be Lancelot. He even had Lancelot's own helmet and armor. He had come to DSA with Squint and Knuckle, who pretended to be his squires. They had tried to steal Mordred's gold!

But Erica, Angus, and Wiglaf had caught them. Now the thieves were locked in the DSA dungeon. And Wiglaf and his friends were about to set off on a quest to save Sir Lancelot— if only Mordred would stop talking!

At last Mordred paused. He checked the sundial he wore on his wrist. "Where the dickens is that monk?" he muttered. "How long can it take to write a few hundred flyers?"

"Sir!" cried Erica. "Please! We must be off!"

"Yes, yes," Mordred said. "By the way, I had Frypot put sandwiches in your packs."

"What kind, Uncle?" Angus asked eagerly.

"Your favorite kind!" Mordred boomed.

Angus's face lit up. "Oh, joy!" he cried. "Bacon-cheese boarburgers!"

"Well, no..." Mordred said. "Lumpen pudding sandwiches. They'll stick to your ribs."

Wiglaf groaned. He hated lumpen pudding! One bite of the mossy green glop made him lose his appetite.

Just then Brother Dave, the DSA librarian, burst out of the gatehouse. He ran down the drawbridge toward them as fast as his robes would allow. He carried a tall stack of parchments.

"Here you are, sir," the monk said breathlessly. He handed Mordred the flyers.

Mordred checked one. Then he smiled and held up a flyer for all to see:

The Official Dragon Slayers' Academy Quiz

Are you a lad? ☐yes ☐no ☐not so sure

Can you get your hands on seven pennies?

☐yes ☐no ☐one way or another

If you answered YES to at least two of these questions, congratulations! *YOU* have what it takes to become a student at DRAGON SLAYERS' ACADEMY! Our graduates slay dragons and get rich. Invest in your future—sign up today!

—Mordred the Marvelous, Headmaster

"Here, nephew," Mordred said. "Hand these out to folks you meet on your quest."

"But my pack is so heavy," said Angus.

"Then you take them, Eric," Mordred said.

Mordred had no idea that Erica would flunk the "lad" part of his quiz. She dressed as a boy so she could go to the all-boys DSA. Wiglaf was the only student who knew her secret. She was Princess Erica, daughter of

Queen Barb and King Ken. Erica thought that if Mordred discovered she was a girl, he would kick her out of DSA. But Wiglaf knew better. After all, Princess Erica was worth a fortune in the thing Mordred loved best—gold.

"My pack is full, sir," Erica said. "I have a first-aid kit for Sir Lancelot—just in case. And I have Sir Lancelot's helmet, which I shall give him after we save him."

Save him, Wiglaf thought. *But how?* He felt a small knot of worry forming in his stomach.

"Wiglaf," Mordred growled, "take the flyers."

Wiglaf knew better than to argue. He shoved the flyers into his pack. They weighed a ton! But surely *now* they could be off.

He felt his pet pig, Daisy, nudge him.

"Iglaf-way!" she said. She had spoken Pig Latin ever since the wizard Zelnoc cast a speech spell on her. "Ease-play! Ake-tay ee-may ith-way ou-yay!"

Wiglaf bent down and hugged his pig. "It is too long a journey for a short-legged pig."

"Ee-may?" Daisy gasped. "Ort-shay egged-lay?"

"You would slow us down on our quest," Wiglaf said. "And I do not want you to be in danger."

"I-yay ive-lay or-fay anger-day!" Daisy said.

"Be a good pig while I am gone," Wiglaf said.

"Ood-gay ig-pay, ooey-phay!" Daisy grumbled. And she trotted off in a huff.

"Do not dilly-dally," Mordred was saying. "Get the reward and get back here."

"Yes, Uncle Mordred," said Angus.

"Off you go then," Mordred said. "Scram!"

"Forward, march!" cried Erica. She started off toward Huntsman's Path.

Wiglaf's heart was glad as he marched behind her. Sounds of cheering rang in his ears. At last, they were off on their quest!

Chapter 2

Wiglaf smiled as he marched. Rolling hills stretched out before him. The Swamp River bubbled in the distance. He took a breath. He smelled adventure in the air! Or—was it only the fishy smell of the river? Oh, what did it matter? He was on a quest!

Erica struck up a questing song:
"We're off to save Sir Lancelot!
The bravest knight who ever got
Upon his horse and gave a swat
To knaves hatching a wicked plot
Or dragons breathing fires hot!
Oh, somewhere north of Camelot

We'll find that knight Sir Lancelot!
We'll save him, he'll say, 'Thanks a lot!'
Sir Lancelot...hooray!"

Wiglaf and Angus picked up the tune. They sang as they marched. And marched.

At last, the sun set and it grew cool.

"I cannot walk another step!" Angus moaned. "Let us camp for the night."

Erica put up the quick-pitch tent she'd ordered from the Sir Lancelot Fan Club catalog. Wiglaf and Angus struggled to put up an old tent of Mordred's. Then Erica lit a fire. They sat around it, nibbling their lumpen pudding sandwiches.

Wiglaf began to worry about Sir Lancelot. How could they save him from a witch's spell? The knot in his stomach seemed to grow. Or was that just a lump of lumpen pudding?

"I hope," he said at last, "that Morgana le Fay is not a very powerful sort of witch."

"Are you jesting?" Erica exclaimed.

"Morgana is half sister to King Arthur. She is the *most* powerful witch in the world!"

"Egad!" cried Wiglaf. "Then how can we hope to save Lancelot from her spell?"

"I have it," Angus said. "Let's turn back!"

"Never!" Erica folded her arms.

"We shall need help," Wiglaf said. "Maybe we should summon Zelnoc."

Erica frowned. "That mixed-up old wizard?"

"Mixed-up magic is better than none," Wiglaf said. Then he summoned the wizard by chanting his name backwards three times: "Conlez! Conlez! Conlez!"

A shooting star blazed across the night sky. Wiglaf watched it grow bigger. It looked like...what? Not a wizard in a blue star-speckled robe. But...a wizard clutching a ratty blue towel around his middle!

"You again, Wiglip!" Zelnoc cried as he touched down beside the campfire. Except for the towel, he was bare. And dripping with white suds. "Can't I take a simple bubble bath without your Conlez, Conlez, Conlez?"

"So sorry, sir," Wiglaf managed.

"I should have turned off my summoner before I got in the tub," Zelnoc mumbled. "*Brr.* I must take care not to catch cold." Zelnoc raised one hand in the air and cried, "Robe, please!"

At once, a blue terry-cloth robe appeared and wrapped itself around him. A sash tied itself around his waist. His towel fell to the ground.

"Did I say *bath*robe?" Zelnoc muttered. "I did not! But...it is cozy." He shrugged. "Well, Wiglamp? What's the problem now?"

"We are on a quest, sir," Wiglaf said.

"A quest to save Sir Lancelot," Erica added.

"A witch has put a curse on him," Angus said.

"Can you help us, sir?" asked Wiglaf.

"Do dragons have scales?" Zelnoc asked.

"Do warthogs have warts? Of course I can help. A wizard is far more powerful than a witch. Now, which witch is it?"

"Morgana le Fay," answered Wiglaf.

"Oops!" said Zelnoc. "I make a rule not to mess with her. She's *mean*."

"Why...how mean is she?" asked Wiglaf.

"Morgana is so mean," Zelnoc said, "that if a rattlesnake bites her, the rattler dies."

Wiglaf's eyes grew wide.

"Morgana is so mean," Zelnoc said, "that her favorite dish is baked baby unicorn chops."

"No!" Angus gasped.

"Morgana is so mean," Zelnoc added, "that on a whim, she turned my grandpappy into a bat! Take it from me, leave Morgana alone!"

"But she's put a curse on Sir Lancelot!" Erica cried. "We have to help him!"

"No offense," Zelnoc said. "But the three of you are small, powerless, and, from the looks of things, not too bright. How do you think you can go up against the Queen of Mean?"

"That's why we called you, sir," Wiglaf said.

"Can't help you on this one," Zelnoc said. "I'll be getting back to my bath now. Ta-ta!"

"Wait!" Wiglaf cried. "Did you not tell me once that wizards must help the helpless?"

"Oh, toads and toadstools!" Zelnoc cried. "Wizard Rule #762. You've got me there. All right. I'll think of something while I'm in the tub. Then I'll be back. Now, toodle-oo!"

"Hold it, Zelnoc!" Erica called. "How do we know you'll be back?"

"I'm a wizard of my word," Zelnoc said. "But if you doubt it, here!" He raised his right hand in the air. He pointed at a ring on his left little finger. It floated off his pinkie and hovered in the air in front of the wizard.

"Grab it, Wicklaf!" Zelnoc said.

Wiglaf reached out. As he did, the ring slipped onto his thumb, tightening around it.

"My grandpappy gave me that ring for my 105th birthday," Zelnoc said. "I'll be back to get it. So, may your quest be a success. May good win over evil and all that. But don't summon me, boy. You won't get through."

With that, Zelnoc jumped onto his towel. The towel stiffened. With a *whoosh!* he sailed off into the night winds until he vanished.

Wiglaf stared at the wizard's ring. He was sorry to see that its stone was mossy green. Just the color of lumpen pudding.

The fire had burned low. The three began unrolling their sleeping bags.

Wiglaf stopped midroll. He listened. Something was rustling in the bushes.

"Now what?" Erica whispered. She drew her sword. She charged toward the noise. "Come out, villain!" she cried. She beat the bushes with her sword. "Come out now! Or I shall smite you! Your blood shall flow like a river!"

The thought of such a bloody scene made Wiglaf feel woozy.

"Come out, I say—yikes!" Erica yelped.

Wiglaf and Angus ran to her side.

Erica stood frozen to the spot. Her sword was pointed at the nose of a large dog.

"Don't hurt it!" Angus cried. He pushed Erica's sword away.

Wiglaf saw that the skin on the dog's big face was folded in many wrinkles. His floppy ears hung down below his chin.

"Why, it's a bloodhound," he said.

"Go away," Erica told the dog.

The bloodhound answered with a "Woof!" Then he jumped up, putting his paws on Erica's shoulders. He licked her face.

"Ugh!" Erica cried. She pushed him down and wiped dog drool from her cheek.

"He likes you," Angus told Erica.

The dog thumped his tail happily.

"I don't like him," Erica said. She turned and

dove into her tent. She tied the tent flaps together. "There!" she muttered. "Dog proof!"

"Come here, boy," Wiglaf said. "What's your name, I wonder?" He and Angus coaxed the dog over to the campfire.

"His coat shines red in the firelight," Angus said, scratching the dog's chin. "We could call him Rufus. It means 'red-hair.'"

"Don't name him!" Erica shouted from inside her tent. "We aren't keeping him!"

"Why not?" Angus said. "Rufus can come on the quest with us and be our brave protector."

"No way!" called Erica.

"Bloodhounds are good trackers," Wiglaf said. "Rufus can sniff Sir Lancelot's scent from his helmet and lead us to him."

Erica stuck her head halfway out of her tent. She eyed the dog uncertainly.

Rufus leaped up and bounded over to her.

"Yiii!" Erica cried. She pulled her head into the tent before Rufus could lick her again.

"Are you afraid of Rufus?" Wiglaf asked.

"Me?" Erica said from inside the tent. "How can you think *I* could fear a dog?"

"Because you're hiding," Wiglaf answered.

"I'm not hiding," Erica said. "I'm resting."

"Nah," said Angus. "You're scared."

Erica was quiet. Then, in a small voice, she said, "Well, what if I am?"

Angus and Wiglaf clapped their hands over their mouths, trying not to laugh. Could fearless Erica really be scared of a *dog*?

"It's not funny!" Erica snarled. "And if you *ever* tell anyone, I'll whack off your heads!"

Instantly, Angus and Wiglaf stopped laughing. They swore to keep her secret.

"We have a long march tomorrow," Erica said in her usual commanding voice. "Good night!"

Rufus lay down outside Erica's tent. He put his head on his paws and closed his eyes.

Wiglaf and Angus crawled into their tent. Soon, all four questers were asleep.

Wiglaf was the first to wake the next morning. He stepped out of the tent. He saw that Rufus was chewing on...

"My boot!" Wiglaf cried, grabbing it.

Rufus seemed to think tug-the-boot was a fine game. He held on tightly.

Erica's head popped out of her tent. "What's all the racket?" she said sleepily.

Rufus dropped the boot. He ran over to Erica and began licking her face.

"Get away, dog!" Erica wailed. "Begone!"

Angus crawled out of the big tent. "Rufus likes you," he told Erica again.

Erica wiped her cheek. "Drooling fool!"

Wiglaf picked up his boot. It was slimy but not badly chewed. He pulled it on. After a breakfast of berries, they packed up.

"If the dog can track Sir Lancelot, he can come with us," Erica said. She gave Angus a

length of rope from her tool belt. "Here. Use this for a leash. And keep him away from me."

Angus looped the rope loosely around the dog's neck. Rufus didn't seem to mind.

Erica took Sir Lancelot's helmet from her pack. She handed it to Wiglaf. He held the helmet under Rufus's nose.

"Get the scent, boy," Wiglaf said.

Rufus sniffed the helmet. Then he threw back his head and let out a howl. He put his nose to the ground and began tracking.

"Sir Lancelot, here we come!" Angus cried.

The questers had to run through the Dark Forest to keep up with Rufus. Wiglaf had no idea where they were going. But clearly, Rufus was following the trail of Sir Lancelot's scent.

They followed the dog all morning long. At last Rufus led them onto a bridge that arched over the Swamp River. Wiglaf frowned. This bridge...it looked familiar.

"Stop!" Erica cried suddenly when they were halfway across. "Turn back!"

"Just what *I've* been saying!" Angus said.

"No! That's not what I mean," Erica cried. "Look where we are! This is the troll bridge!"

Then up from the churning river waters popped the head of a horrible troll.

"Freeze or I'll eat you!" roared the troll.

The questers froze. Nobody moved a muscle.

"Very nice." The troll smiled, showing shiny sharklike teeth. "Of course," he added, "I'm going to eat you anyway."

Chapter 3

he troll hopped up onto the bridge.

"I'll have *you* for breakfast," he said, pointing a hairy finger at Angus.

"No..." Angus whimpered. "Please, no!"

The troll pointed at Wiglaf. "You for lunch."

Wiglaf trembled with fear.

"You for dinner," the troll told Erica. "And doggy for dessert!"

The troll licked his lips. "I am one lucky Trog today!"

"Trog?" Erica said. "Do you not remember us? We have crossed your bridge before."

Trog scratched his ear. "You're not those billy goats, are you?"

"No," said Erica. "We gave you cabbage soup."

Trog's yellow eyes lit up. "Oh, yummy soup!" He smiled. Then his smile faded. "But it gave me a bad tummy ache!"

"Some batches turn out better than others," Wiglaf admitted. "My mother—"

"No talk of mothers!" Trog cried suddenly. "My mommy was kidnapped! Now I have to do all my own cooking." Big tears rolled down his cheeks. "And I am *not* a good cook."

"We can cook something for you," Angus said quickly. "Then you won't have to eat us."

Trog wiped his nose on his sleeve. He pointed to the mouth of a cave on the far side of the bridge. "March!" he said.

The questers set off for the cave. Wiglaf was worried. Did Angus know how to cook? He had never said anything about it.

Just inside the mouth of the cave, Rufus stopped. He covered his nose with his paws.

Wiglaf wanted to cover his nose, too. The cave smelled like garbage and dirty dishes.

Trog lit a torch. Indeed, the cave *was* filled with garbage and dirty dishes. Pots and pans encrusted with glop were stacked to the cave ceiling.

Trog pointed to Angus. "You cook." He pointed to Wiglaf and Erica. "You and you. Clean up."

Erica gasped. "You don't mean wash dishes!"

Trog nodded. "Do it," he said.

"No, no," Erica said. "You see, Trog, we are trying to prove our bravery and become knights. That is why we are on a quest to save Sir Lancelot from Morgana le Fay."

"Morgana?" Trog cried. "Morgana kid-napped my mommy! She put a spell on her and took her away!" More tears splashed out of his eyes.

"Well, after we save Sir Lancelot from Morgana," Erica said, "we'll save your mommy."

Trog sniffed. "I am big and strong," he said. "I have a spiked club. You are small and weak. Your swords look like toothpicks. I could not save my mommy. So how can you?"

"Uh..." said Erica. "It's hard to explain."

Trog rolled his yellow eyes.

"Listen, Trog," Angus said. "I don't see much to cook around here. Try this." He handed the troll one of Frypot's sandwiches.

The troll sank his sharky teeth into it.

"Mmmm," Trog said, licking his scaly lips. "Tastes like lumpen pudding."

"It *is* lumpen pudding," Angus said.

"Mommy used to make yummy lumpen pudding," Trog said. Then came the tears again. "Break the spell on my mommy," he wailed. "Send her home to her Troggy. She's been gone so long!"

"We shall, Trog," Erica promised.

"My mommy likes human children," Trog sniffed.

"I am sure we shall like her, too," Angus said.

"No," Trog said. "Mommy likes human children baked in a pie. She might eat you before she knows you're trying to help her."

"I see." Wiglaf thought fast. "Can you write your mommy a letter, Trog?" he asked. "We could show it to her. Then she will know that we are your...uh, friends."

A smile spread across Trog's face.

"I have parchment." Wiglaf took a DSA flyer from his pack. He turned it over.

"Here is a quill and an ink pot," Erica said. She unclipped them from her tool belt.

Trog grabbed the quill. He dunked it in the ink. Then he set to work. He wrote for quite some time. "There!" he said at last. "Done."

The troll thrust the parchment at Wiglaf.

Wiglaf's heart sank when he saw it. The letter was nothing but blots and scribbles! It would never save them.

"Take it to my mommy," the troll said. "She won't eat you when she reads this."

Wiglaf nodded. With a heavy heart, he folded the parchment and put it in his pocket.

Angus gave Trog another lumpen pudding sandwich.

Then Erica said, "Good-bye, Trog." And she led the questers out of the cave.

Wiglaf nearly tripped over Rufus on his way out. The dog lay just outside the mouth of the cave, chewing on something. Angus grabbed Rufus's rope, and the questers ran from the troll cave into the welcome fresh air.

In the daylight, Wiglaf saw that Rufus was carrying something in his teeth. It was a limp, drool-soaked piece of leather that looked as if it might once have been a troll boot.

Chapter 4

he questers ran far from the troll cave. They did not want to be around when Trog discovered that one of his boots was missing. At last they stopped. Erica handed Sir Lancelot's helmet to Wiglaf.

Wiglaf held the helmet under the bloodhound's nose. "Get the scent, Rufus," he said.

"I hope the stink of the troll cave hasn't ruined his sniffer," Angus said.

Rufus howled loudly. Then he began sniffing down a trail, leading the questers on.

"Camelot!" cried Erica. "Here we come!"

Again, the questers followed Rufus for mile after mile. It cheered them to sing their questing song as they followed the hound.

"We're off to save Sir Lancelot!
The bravest knight who ever got
Upon his horse and gave a swat..."

Wiglaf had never been to Camelot. And he knew better than to doubt a bloodhound's nose. But this area of the Dark Forest looked remarkably like the outskirts of his home-town, Pinwick. And Pinwick was nowhere near Camelot.

Zounds! thought Wiglaf as they passed a gnarled oak. *That looks like my favorite boyhood climbing tree.*

On they ran.

Egad! thought Wiglaf as he spotted a bro-ken-down shack high on a hill. *That looks like the shack I used to see when my father sent me across the river to hoe the cabbage fields.*

It was afternoon before Rufus stopped. He sniffed the air and let out a chilling wail.

"Rufus?" said Angus. "Is Lancelot nearby?"

The hound bounded forward. His rope

jerked out of Angus's hand. Rufus raced up the hill, dragging the rope behind him.

"Rufus!" called Angus. "Wait for me, boy!"

But the bloodhound never looked back. He shot like an arrow to the top of the hill and disappeared from view.

"Come on!" cried Erica. "Do you not see? The dog is leading us to our knight!" She cupped her hands to her mouth and called, "We are coming to save you, Sir Lancelot!"

The questers raced up the hill after Rufus. Wiglaf thought he heard someone yelling. He could just make out the words. They sounded like *Let go of me, you crazy beast!*

Suddenly, Rufus appeared on the crest of the hill. He had sunk his teeth into a man's pant leg. He was pulling the man down the hill.

"Oh, poor Sir Lancelot!" Erica exclaimed. "Too bad he is not wearing his armor. I must ready the first-aid kit."

Wiglaf shielded his eyes from the late-afternoon sun. Here was the handsome knight at last! Wiglaf saw his flowing mane of dark hair, his famously white teeth.

"Untooth me, hound!" the knight yelped, "or I'll skin you and make myself a vest!"

"Morgana's spell must cause him to speak so harshly," Erica observed.

Rufus kept his jaws clamped firmly on Sir Lancelot's pant leg. He tugged him, kicking and fighting, down the hill to the questers.

Erica fell to one knee. She bowed before the world's most perfect knight.

"Good, Rufus!" Angus said, kneeling down.

Wiglaf dropped to his knees, too. But he kept his eyes on Sir Lancelot. Morgana's spell must have changed him greatly. For the knight looked scruffy and dirty and kind of...short.

"Leon?" Wiglaf said. "It's you, isn't it?"

At the sound of that name, Erica and Angus jumped up.

"Speak, man!" Erica cried. "Are you Leon?"

"Of course I am!" Leon replied. He broke into a smile as he recognized the questers. "Well, well, if it isn't the three little tattletales from the dragon school!"

Angus smacked himself on the forehead. "Leon had on Sir Lancelot's helmet!" he cried. "Rufus picked up Leon's scent instead of Lancelot's!"

Rufus proudly thumped his tail.

Erica frowned. "But you and Squint and Knuckle were locked in the DSA dungeon."

Leon grinned. "Yes. Master X was all ready to chop off our heads." Master X was the DSA weapons teacher. "But first, he wanted to test the sharpness of his blade. And he cut the dickens out of his thumb. A bloody mess, it was."

Wiglaf began to feel dizzy.

"Master X fainted dead away," said Leon.

"No!" cried Erica.

"Oh yes he did," said Leon. "We sawed off our ropes with his axe. We were on our steeds and gone in no time." He looked behind the questers and added, "Were we not, Squint?"

Wiglaf whirled around. There stood Squint and Knuckle Squeegee—the butchers of Pinwick!

"Indeed we were," said Knuckle. "All right, men. Let's take these runts back to the butcher shop. One of them can write a ransom note for us to take to DSA." He grinned. "Looks like we're going to get Mordred's gold after all!"

"Your plan won't work," Angus told Knuckle. "Uncle Mordred shan't give up his gold for us."

"Uncle?" Squint cried. "You're *family*? Oh, Mordred will pay all right!"

"You don't know him," Erica said. "Mordred is greedy. His gold means everything to him."

"Come on, runts," Leon said. "March to the butcher shop. Hup, two, three!"

They marched. Erica bravely struck up their questing song. Wiglaf and Angus joined in:

"We're off to save Sir Lancelot!
The bravest knight who ever got
Upon his horse and gave a swat
To knaves hatching a wicked plot..."

When the song ended, Knuckle cried, "Did you hear that, Squint?"

"I did, indeed, Knuckle!" cried Squint.

They burst out laughing. Then Knuckle hooked elbows with Squint and sang:

"We're off to save Sir Lancelot!
Sir Lancelot! Sir Lancelot!
The knight who wets his pants a lot!
Sir Lancelot...hey, hey!"

"Make no fun of him!" Erica cried.

"Aw!" said Knuckle. "Are you going to tell the dumb cluck what I said?"

"You don't want to ruffle his feathers!" warned Squint. And they doubled over laughing.

Whatever are they laughing about? Wiglaf wondered.

They reached the butcher shop. Squint shoved Wiglaf and the others inside. P.U.! It smelled even *worse* than the troll cave.

"Hey, where's Rufus?" Angus asked.

Wiglaf looked around. "He must have run off."

"That is *so* like a dog!" Erica exclaimed.

"You! Mordred's nephew!" Knuckle said. "Write a ransom note. And make it a real tear-jerker."

Wiglaf handed Angus one of Mordred's DSA flyers. He had to admit the things were coming in handy. Erica gave Angus the quill and ink. And Angus wrote the note.

When he finished, Leon said, "Read it!" Angus obeyed.

"Dear Uncle Mordred,

Kindly give all your gold to the bearer of this note. Or I fear you shall never see me again.

Please, Uncle! You can always get more gold. But loving nephews are hard to find.

Your very loving nephew,

Me, Angus

P.S. Eric and Wiglaf are kidnapped, too. So you will get three for the price of one!"

"That's the ticket!" Knuckle cried. He snatched the parchment from Angus. He rolled it up and handed it to Squint. "Take this to the dragon school, brother," he said.

"Why me?" said Squint. "I don't want to go back there. I'll run into Master X!"

Knuckle turned to Leon. "You take it."

"Oh, no," Leon said. "Master X isn't getting a second chance to lop off *my* head. Besides, I have a blister on my big toe and—" Leon stopped. He chewed on a hangnail thoughtfully. "Uh...on second thought, I'm your man, Knuckle," he said. "My blister isn't so bad. I shall go to DSA."

Knuckle eyed Leon suspiciously.

"I shall definitely come back with all the gold," said Leon, smiling sweetly. "Trust me!"

"No way," said Knuckle. "I must go myself."

Leon shook his head. "But I don't trust *you*!"

"Looks like we must all go together," Squint put in. "And I say we wear our disguises!"

"Ha! Master X will never recognize us!" said Squint. "But...what about the runts?"

"Tie 'em up and lock 'em in," said Leon.

Squint grinned. He tied the questers' hands tightly behind their backs.

"May good win over evil!" Erica shouted as Squint shoved them down on the hard dirt floor.

The thieves only laughed. Then Knuckle threw open a big trunk. The thieves took out scarves and shawls. They took out bonnets, too.

The questers stared openmouthed as the thieves got dressed up.

"Well?" said Leon. He hooked a pail over his arm and twirled for the questers. "Have you ever seen three such lovely milkmaids?"

"Milkmaids?" cried Erica. "You are joking!"

"Why, you little..." milkmaid Leon began.

"Pay no attention to the runt, Leon," said milkmaid Knuckle. "Come! Let us be off."

Squint grabbed the ransom note. "Let us be off to milk Mordred of his gold!"

Chuckling, the three milkmaids skipped out, locking the door behind them.

"Oh, woe!" Angus cried. "We'll be tied up for hours until they get back."

"Ha!" scoffed Erica. "They shan't come back. Once they have the gold, why should they?"

"Double woe!" cried Angus. "Are we doomed to die here?"

"Oh, stop whining," Erica snapped. "If we can't get loose, Wiglaf will summon Zelnoc."

"But I can't," Wiglaf said. "Zelnoc said he was turning off his summoner. Remember?"

"We must not give up hope," Erica said.

"Why not?" asked Angus as the daylight faded.

Erica thought for a moment. "Rats may come in the night and gnaw off our ropes," she said.

Wiglaf swallowed. This was a grim hope.

Scratch. Scratch.

What was that? Wiglaf held his breath.

"Help!" Angus cried. "The rats have come!"

Wiglaf squinted. In the dim light, it looked as if a patch of the dirt floor was caving in, making a hole. Something poked up through the hole. Wiglaf's eyes grew wide.

"Look there!" Angus cried. "A nose! It's the nose of the world's biggest rat!"

"You dolt!" Erica cried. "That's no rat!"

Wiglaf blinked. It was—

"Rufus!" he cried joyfully.

Rufus poked his whole head up out of the hole. He worked the rest of his body out, too.

"Over here, dog!" Erica called.

Rufus bounded over to her. She scooted around and held out her tied-up hands.

"Chew on the rope," she ordered. "Chew!"

Rufus understood. He took the ropes that bound her wrists in his teeth. He began to gnaw. At last Erica slid one hand free. She flung the rope from her other hand.

"Not bad," she told Rufus. "For a dog."

Erica lit her mini-torch. Then she quickly untied Wiglaf and Angus. They hugged Rufus.

"You saved us, boy!" Angus cried.

Erica tried the door. But it was locked from the outside. So one by one, they wormed their way through Rufus's tunnel. Wiglaf was the last to get out. How good it felt to be free!

"Onward to Camelot!" Erica cried.

And in the moonlight, the questers set off.

Chapter 5

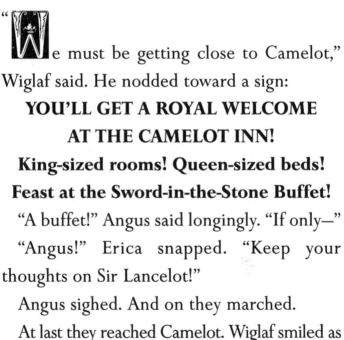

e must be getting close to Camelot," Wiglaf said. He nodded toward a sign:

**YOU'LL GET A ROYAL WELCOME
AT THE CAMELOT INN!**
King-sized rooms! Queen-sized beds!
Feast at the Sword-in-the-Stone Buffet!

"A buffet!" Angus said longingly. "If only—"

"Angus!" Erica snapped. "Keep your thoughts on Sir Lancelot!"

Angus sighed. And on they marched.

At last they reached Camelot. Wiglaf smiled as he saw colorful banners flapping in the breeze. And so many people!

They made their way to King Arthur's castle.

Erica yanked on the castle bellpull. A skinny young servant opened the door.

"Greetings, page!" Erica said boldly. "We should like a word with King Arthur."

Wiglaf smiled. Erica was acting like the haughty princess she really was!

"And what would the likes of you be wanting with the king?" the page asked.

"We are knights-in-training. We have come to save Sir Lancelot," Erica explained.

"You and many others," the page said. "But come in. Bring your dog, too. Most of the knights are out questing today. King Arthur will be glad to have company."

The page led them into the main hall. Wiglaf had heard of the great round table. And there it was! But today only three tattered knights sat around it. One had his arm in a sling. Another had a bandage over one ear. A pair of crutches leaned against the chair of the third. Beside them sat a white-bearded man wearing a crown. It was King Arthur!

The page bowed. "King Arthur, sir!" he said. "May I present three knights-in-training and their noble beast."

Wiglaf, Erica, and Angus fell to their knees. Rufus lay down and bowed his head.

"Sire!" Erica said, jumping up. "We are on a quest to save Sir Lancelot."

"Ah," said King Arthur. "Sir Gareth tried to save Lancelot." He nodded toward the knight with the crutches. "Did you not, Gareth?"

"I did indeed, sire," Sir Gareth answered. "That is how I lost my left leg."

Wiglaf gasped.

"Sir Balyn also rode out to save Sir Lancelot," King Arthur said, pointing to a second knight.

"True enough, sire," said Sir Balyn. "That is how I lost my left ear."

Wiglaf's heart began to pound with fear.

"Sir Geoffrey," King Arthur said to the third knight. "Did you, too, quest after Lancelot?"

The knight with his arm in a sling nodded. "That is how I lost my left hand, sire," he said.

Wiglaf swallowed. He had no wish to lose his left hand. Or leg. Or his left anything!

King Arthur raised an eyebrow. "Are you three *sure* you wish to quest after Lance?"

"No!" cried Angus.

"Yes, we are!" Erica said. "We *shall* save Sir Lancelot if it is the last thing we do!"

"It may well be," said Sir Gareth.

The other knights nodded.

Wiglaf began to tremble. He was terrified!

"Excuse me, your highness," he managed. "What makes this quest so dangerous?"

"My sister, Morgana," King Arthur answered simply. "She's put a curse on Lance, you know."

"We fear her not!" Erica said.

"No?" King Arthur raised his other eyebrow. "Well, I fear her. Morgana is *mean*. Made my childhood a misery, always trying out her spells on me. Once when I was small, she told me to close my eyes and something good would turn up. So I closed my eyes. And Morgana turned my favorite teddy bear into a turnip." The king shook his head. "Morgana laughed herself silly. Kept saying, 'Do you get it, Artie? Something will *turn up—turnip*!'" He sighed. "Bedtime just wasn't the same after that, snuggling with a turnip."

"But what about Sir Lancelot?" asked Erica. "Someone must save him!"

The king looked hard at the questers. "You do not look like much of a match for Morgana," he said. "But looks can be deceiving. So I shall wish you good luck. Percy?" He beckoned to his page. "I'll wager these questers are hungry."

"Yes, sir!" Angus said loudly.

"See if there is any roasted duck left from lunch," King Arthur went on. "Give them some spiced apples and those tasty sausages."

"Thank you, sire!" Angus cried.

Percy led the questers out of the banquet hall. He asked them to wait outside the kitchen. He hurried off. He came back in a moment, carrying three small bags.

"There were no leftovers," he said. "But the cook wrapped up some tarts for you to take with you on your quest. Here you go."

"What kind of tarts?" asked Angus eagerly.

"Lumpen pudding," Percy replied.

"No!" cried all the questers.

"That's gratitude for you!" Percy snapped.

"We have eaten nothing but lumpen pudding for many days," Wiglaf explained.

"Oh." Percy looked very sorry for the questers. "Perhaps I can help you in another way. Shall I give you something of Sir Lancelot's to help your bloodhound track him?"

"Oh, yes!" Erica exclaimed.

The page went off again. He came back and handed Erica a brown velvet bag.

"What is inside?" Erica asked breathlessly.

"Lance's most prized possession," Percy said. "He used to spend hours admiring what he saw in it. Good luck!" he added. And he hurried off.

"Open the drawstrings, Wiglaf!" Erica ordered. "Perhaps it is a book of chivalry."

Wiglaf loosened the strings. He reached into the sack. All the questers held their breath as he pulled out the treasured item.

"Huh?" said Wiglaf. He held something round and shiny. "But what is it?"

"Don't you see?" Erica cried. "Percy has given us Sir Lancelot's mirror!"

Chapter 6

he questers left Camelot. They walked through the Darker Forest to the edge of the Darkest Forest. Erica lit her mini-torch. Angus gripped Rufus's rope tightly.

Wiglaf held out Sir Lancelot's mirror. "Get the scent, Rufus!" he said. "Lead us to him!"

Rufus sniffed the mirror and howled. He put his nose to the ground and took off.

Wiglaf quickly stuffed the mirror into his pack. Then the questers ran after the dog into the Darkest Forest.

Rufus stopped suddenly. On the path Wiglaf saw a knight's glove.

Erica picked it up. It was made of metal mesh. SL was stamped onto the cuff.

"SL! This must belong to *him*!" Erica cried. "Oh, Sir Lancelot, where are you?"

Erica heard no answer. She lovingly tucked the glove into her pack. On they went.

Before long, Erica's torch lit a sign beside the path. It said:

PRIVATE PROPERTY OF ME, MORGANA LE FAY!
GO HOME!
DON'T EVEN THINK ABOUT TRESPASSING!

"Okay," Angus said. "I won't."

"Fiddlesticks," said Erica. On they went.

They soon came to another sign. It said:

ARE YOU STILL HERE?
GET OUT OF MY FOREST.
AND I MEAN NOW!

"Let's goooooo!" Angus wailed.

"Don't be a ninny," Erica scoffed.

The questers pressed on.

The next sign said: YOU'LL BE SORRY!

"These signs mean nothing!" Erica said. "Morgana is only trying to scare us."

"She has done it!" Angus said. He stopped, and yanked on the rope. Rufus stopped, too. "Let's vote. I say we go back!"

"Wiglaf?" Erica said. "What's your vote?"

Wiglaf was scared. But he very much wanted the quest to succeed so that he could be a hero. And for another reason.

"If we go back without a reward," Wiglaf said, "Mordred will throw us into the dungeon."

"But if we go on," Angus said, "we'll end up dead. I much prefer a cold, damp dungeon."

Rufus had been sitting at Angus's side. Now the dog sprang to his feet. Angus was startled. He dropped the rope, and Rufus ran off.

"Not again!" Angus cried, running after him.

Erica and Wiglaf ran, too. They found Rufus standing before a circle of torches. Each one burned with an eerie blue flame.

"Magic is here," Erica whispered. "The dog fears to go beyond the circle of blue light."

Whoosh! Wiglaf looked up. He saw a giant bat swooping down at him.

"Yikes!" he cried. He ducked. He covered his head with his hands.

The bat hovered over the questers, flapping its wings. "Go back!" it screamed. "Private party! Not invited! Go back!"

"Right!" Angus said. "Let's go!"

The flapping stopped. Wiglaf dared to look up. The bat hung by its toes from a tree branch. Its wings were wrapped around its body like a cape. It stared at Wiglaf.

"What's on your thumb?" the bat asked.

"Only a small wart, sir," Wiglaf said. He glanced at his hand. "Oh, you mean the ring?"

"Right," said the bat. "Give it here."

Wiglaf twisted and tugged at the ring. But he could not pull it off.

"Sorry, sir," he told the bat. "It's stuck."

"Where did you get it?" the bat asked.

"A wizard gave it to me," Wiglaf answered.

"Zelnoc?" asked the bat.

"Why, yes," Wiglaf replied. "He gave it to me as a promise that he would return and—" He had a sudden thought. "Say, are you..."

"Zelnoc's grandpappy," the bat said. "That's me. I was a wizard once. Zamster the Amazing. Now I'm Morgana's watch bat." He sighed again. "I'm supposed to keep party crashers away."

"Will you let us pass?" Erica asked the bat. "For we are on a quest to save Sir Lancelot!"

"No one's been able to save him so far," the bat said. "But go ahead. Have a try. The party's about to begin. Morgana might not notice a few extra guests. On the other hand, you never know."

Wiglaf did not like the sound of that. But he followed Erica as she stepped between two blue-flame torches.

"Don't get caught!" the bat called after

them. "Morgana will clip my wings if she finds out I've helped you."

The questers hurried through the forest. At last they saw a light far away. They stopped. Erica took Wiglaf's hand. Wiglaf took Angus's hand. Angus held Rufus's rope. Erica put out her torch. Black night covered them.

"May good win over evil!" Angus whispered in a shaky voice. Then together they made their way toward the faraway light.

At last Morgana's palace came into view. It was made of black stone, so it was not easy to see in the dark. A single torch lit the entry.

The questers ducked down behind some bushes and peeked out.

Wiglaf barely made out a weedy garden dotted with dozens of small statues. Beyond it people were lined up outside the palace door.

Well, *people* was not exactly the word.

"It's a costume party, right?" Angus asked.

"I don't think so," Erica answered.

Wiglaf didn't think so either. He saw a sorceress chatting with a warlock. Giants, gnomes, and trolls were grumbling together. At the end of the line stood a grave robber. He looked as if he'd come to the party straight from work.

Wiglaf felt a tap on his shoulder. He whirled around. Two men stood behind him.

"Sorry to bother you," one of them said. "We're the delivery peasants from Squat & Gobble Caterers. You know where we're supposed to take the brew?" He motioned to a cart loaded with wooden barrels.

Wiglaf pointed to the palace.

"Ha! Plain as the nose on my face," said the second peasant. He whistled. "Looks like Morgana's having herself quite a wingding."

"I hear she has a guest of honor tonight," said the first peasant.

"Who's that?" asked Erica.

The first peasant laughed. "Why, it's Sir Lancelot!"

Chapter 7

he delivery peasants began pulling their cart toward the mouth of the cave.

"Quick!" Erica whispered. "Jump in! We can hide in the cart and get into the palace!"

The questers snuck up behind the cart. One by one, they hopped in. Rufus jumped in last.

The delivery peasants never noticed a thing.

"Make way!" they cried to the party guests. "Coming through with the brew!"

The guests parted to let the wagon pass. Before long, Wiglaf heard a gruff voice.

"About time you got here, peasants!" it said.

Wiglaf peeked out of the cart. A big troll guarded the entryway. She wore a red dress that laced up the front. Thin red hair covered her lumpy troll head. Watery yellow eyes peered out of her doughy face. When she talked, she showed her large sharklike teeth.

Wiglaf shuddered.

The party guests were hanging their capes on wall pegs. Wiglaf and the others hopped out of the cart. They kept to the shadows.

The palace entrance had been fitted with an iron gate. A sign over the gate said MAGIC DETECTOR. The troll kept an eye on the party guests as they filed through the gate. Two ogres holding clubs stood behind her.

"How do we get inside?" Erica whispered.

Wiglaf spied the coatrack. "We could put on capes and hats and go as gnomes."

Angus rolled his eyes. But he had no better idea. So one by one, the questers made their way to the rack. Each slipped on a cape and a stocking cap. Angus put a cap on Rufus, too. Then they inched over to the line. As they passed a giant, he growled, "No cutting, gnomes! I was here first."

Wiglaf smiled. The disguises had fooled the giant! He hoped they would fool the troll.

The questers squeezed into the line behind the giant. Wiglaf took a deep breath. He watched as a real gnome stepped up to the magic detector.

"No wands, staffs, or magical doodads of any kind are allowed," the troll growled. "Ms. le Fay likes to be in charge of all magic on her home turf."

The troll began frisking the gnome.

"Hoo ha!" cried the gnome. "That tickles!"

"Quiet!" snapped the troll. "Or I'll tell Ms. le Fay. You know how she loves to turn gnomes into garden ornaments."

The gnome stopped laughing. He walked through the gate. Nothing happened.

"You! Sorceress! You're next," the troll shouted. "Get a move on!"

"Good evening," the sorceress said in a low voice. "*I* have nothing magical. Trust me."

"Walk!" barked the troll.

The sorceress walked through the magic detector. Bells began clanging loudly.

"Shakedown!" yelled the troll. She grabbed the sorceress by the ankles and shook her up and down. A staff, a crystal ball, and several wands fell out of her pockets.

"I'm innocent!" cried the sorceress. "Somebody planted this stuff on me!"

The troll put the sorceress down with a thud. "When I say no magic, I *mean* no magic!"

"Magic schmagic," the sorceress muttered. She smoothed her gown. Then she walked with as much dignity as possible through the magic detector. This time it was silent.

"You can pick up your gear here after the party," said the troll. "Next!"

The giant walked through the gate.

Wiglaf's heart began to pound. They were

next! He watched Erica walk through the magic detector. No bells rang. Then Angus and Rufus walked through without a hitch. Now it was his turn. Wiglaf drew a breath. He stepped through the magic detector.

Bells rang crazily!

Wiglaf froze. He had no magic. Why had he set off the alarm? What should he do? He did the only thing he could think of—he ran!

"Stop in the name of le Fay!" cried the troll.

But Wiglaf kept running down the hallway.

"Take over for me, ogres!" cried the troll. "I'm going to nab this naughty gnome!"

Wiglaf zoomed around a corner. He pressed himself flat against a wall. He hoped the troll would run by without seeing him. But the next thing he knew, rough hands grabbed him by the ankles. The troll flipped him upside down and shook him.

"Ah-ee-eee-ee!" cried Wiglaf.

"Humph! Nothing." The troll put Wiglaf

down. She eyed him suspiciously. "Ah! I see it." She held out a hand. "The ring, please."

Zelnoc's ring! Was it magical? Wiglaf twisted and turned it. But he could not pull it off.

"It is stuck," he said at last. "A wizard gave it to me. I did not know it was magic."

"Oh, sure," said the troll. "Say, what's this?" The troll bent down and picked up a folded piece of parchment from the floor. "It must have fallen out of your pocket."

Trog's scribbles! Wiglaf had forgotten all about them.

The troll looked up from the parchment.

"Trog writes troll nicely for one so young," she said. "But he's not making much sense."

Wiglaf gasped. He should have known! "You're Trog's *mother*!" he exclaimed.

The troll nodded. "That I am. Just listen to what he says." She cleared her throat:

"Dear Mommy,

My friend will give you this letter. He will

break the spell so *you* can come home and cook me billy goat stew. Yum! How I miss it.

Your son, Troggy

P.S. The cave is a mess. Come and clean it!"

The troll frowned. "Spell? What spell?"

"The one Morgana put on you so she could kidnap you," Wiglaf told her.

The troll laughed. "There's no spell. Morgana came by the cave. She said she could use a fine troll like me. Well, I was sick and tired of Trog's *"Mommy, do this! Mommy, cook that!"* I needed a break! And I thought it might be good for Trog to be on his own for a while." The troll shrugged. "Morgana said she'd pay me and buy me new clothes." The troll twirled once to show off her dress. "So I left."

"I see," said Wiglaf.

The troll shook her head. "But all must not be well at home," she said. "Or Trog would never have made friends with a gnome."

"I am, uh, not exactly a gnome." Wiglaf pulled off the stocking cap.

"A human! Mmmm!" The troll licked her scaly lips. "I do love humans."

"Please! Do not eat me!" Wiglaf cried. "Trog and I are friends. Remember?"

"Oh, all right." The troll sighed. "Now you've gone and made me miss Trog. You know," she added, half to herself, "if I sneak out of here tonight, I could be home by dawn."

"Excuse me," said Wiglaf. "But I'd like to go into the ballroom. My friends and I are trying to save Sir Lancelot."

The troll shrugged. "Well, I won't stop you. But steer clear of Morgana," she cautioned. "I don't know what she'll do to you if she catches you. But it won't be nice."

Chapter 8

Wiglaf pulled on his gnome hat. He headed for the ballroom. He found Morgana's party in full swing. Guests stood around drinking goblets of brew. And nibbling cheese and crackers.

In the center of the ballroom was a raised platform. On it Wiglaf saw what looked like a large birdcage covered with a black cloth.

"Wiglaf!" Erica cried as she, Angus, and Rufus rushed over to him. Wiglaf had never been so glad to see his friends.

As he began telling them what had happened with the troll, a gong sounded. The room grew still.

A shower of sparks lit the platform. They faded and a dark-haired woman in a silver robe appeared. Morgana le Fay!

"Welcome, guests!" Morgana's cold smile made Wiglaf shudder. "I have asked you here to show you a world-famous knight."

"Sir Lancelot!" a gnome called out.

Morgana glared at the gnome. "How dare you interrupt!" she cried. She raised her arms toward the gnome. "You'll be nice and quiet from now on!" And she began to chant:

"A noisy gnome annoys me so,

To the garden he must go!"

Yellow sparks shot from Morgana's fingertips. Wiglaf glanced back at the gnome. Morgana had turned him to stone!

Morgana smiled. "Well, well. A new garden ornament!" she said. "Ogres!"

The ogres ran over. They carried the stone gnome out of the ballroom.

"Sir Lancelot is the world's bravest knight," Morgana went on. No one interrupted her. "But that knight now thinks he is..." Morgana smiled coldly. "Well, see for yourselves."

She pulled on a black velvet rope that hung above her head. Slowly the cloth over the cage rose. Inside the cage, a man wearing white long underwear sat on a nest of straw. Wiglaf gasped. It was Sir Lancelot!

The knight sat back on his heels. His hands were tucked into his armpits. He smiled strangely. He had a dazed look in his eyes.

Erica groaned softly. "My poor hero!"

"Lancie?" Morgana crooned.

The knight cocked his head toward her.

"I've put a foul curse on you, sir!" Morgana laughed. "Say a few words for my guests."

Sir Lancelot began to flap his elbows up and down. He stuck out his chin and cackled: *"Bluck-bluck! Bluck-bluck! Cluck-cluck!"*

"No!" Erica moaned.

"Behold Sir Lancelot!" Morgana cried. "The knight who believes he is a chicken!"

Wiglaf groaned. Now he got Morgana's joke. Now he understood what the Squeegees had meant when they said "dumb cluck" and "don't ruffle his feathers." For Morgana had, indeed, put a *fowl* curse upon Sir Lancelot.

Morgana coaxed Sir Lancelot out of his cage. The questers watched in horror. The poor knight kept his knees bent as he waddled onto the platform. He clucked and flapped his elbows.

The party guests clapped. One called out, "Way to go, wicked one!"

Angus sniffled. "What a fate!"

Rufus whimpered.

Erica grew red with anger.

"I have taught him a trick," Morgana said. She picked up some corn kernels from a feed

bag next to the cage. She held the corn above Lance's head. She circled her hand. Sir Lancelot clucked and turned around.

The party guests clapped some more.

"Back in your cage now, sir!" Morgana tossed some corn into the cage. Sir Lancelot dashed in after it. Morgana shut the door behind him. She smiled her icy smile. "Now, feast! Dance! Come up and feed Sir Lancelot. Enjoy yourselves at my Fowl Ball! I must go check on another spell I want to surprise you with, dear party guests. I shall return!" Then *poof!* She vanished in a shower of sparks.

Next, a pair of minstrels strolled onto the platform. They began to sing:

"Oh, Morgana had a ball! E-i-e-i-o!

And at that ball she had a chicken! E-i-e-i-o!

With a cluck-cluck here, and a cluck-cluck..."

"Oh, think, Wiglaf!" Erica whispered. "How can we save Sir Lancelot?"

Wiglaf thought. But his mind was a blank.

Soon a band took the stage.

"It's Lowly Birth!" Angus exclaimed. "I've always wanted to go to one of their concerts!"

Lowly Birth struck up its most famous song, "Serf City." The guests began to dance.

Wiglaf glanced up at Sir Lancelot. A pair of ogres stood by his cage. They looked scary. But they did not look very bright.

"Angus?" Wiglaf whispered. "Do you think you can get the ogres away from the cage?"

"Me?" Angus swallowed. "All right," he managed. "With Rufus's help, I'll try."

Wiglaf nodded. He turned to Erica. "Can you get Sir Lancelot to come out of his cage and then lead him over to the door?"

Erica nodded. "I shall find a way."

Wiglaf nodded again. "I shall get rid of the party guests," he said. "Meet me over by the door. That is where I shall show

Sir Lancelot his mirror. Maybe if he sees himself, it will break the spell. But if it does not, at least we can try to make a run for it."

Wiglaf took Sir Lancelot's mirror from his pack. He slid it under his gnome cloak.

Erica put out her right hand. Angus slapped his hand on top. Wiglaf put his hand on Angus's. Rufus surprised them by adding his paw to the pile. "May good win over evil!" the questers whispered. Then they split up.

Wiglaf pulled his gnome hat down to hide his face. He went up to the grave robber.

"Excuse me, sir," he said in a high gnome-like voice. "Ms. le Fay is having trouble with her new spell. She fears it might explode—"

Before Wiglaf could say another word, the grave robber turned and ran from the room.

One down and fifty or so to go, Wiglaf thought. He walked up to a giant.

Meanwhile, Angus climbed the steps to the platform.

"Hello, ogres," he said. "Ms. le Fay needs some... uh... nettles for her spell. She wants you to go into the Darkest Forest and gather them."

"Now?" asked one ogre.

"Now," Angus said. "Don't worry about Sir Lancelot. I'll guard his cage for you."

"Thanks," the ogres said. Then they picked up their clubs and lumbered off.

It was Erica's turn. She ran onto the platform. She grabbed several handfuls of corn from the feed bag. She stuffed it into her pocket. Then she opened the cage door.

"Come, sir," she said, spreading a trail of corn leading out of the cage. "Out you go."

Sir Lancelot clucked eagerly. A kernel at a time, he ate his way to freedom. Erica tossed corn on the steps. She lured the knight down the steps and onto the dance floor. And she began dancing. She tossed corn while she danced. She moved ever closer to the ballroom door. Sir Lancelot followed where she led, pecking up the corn.

The few party guests that were left glanced at Erica and Lance. But all they saw was a cheeky gnome making sport of Sir Lancelot.

Wiglaf made his way to the ballroom door. Angus hurried over to him.

"I can't find Rufus," Angus whispered.

"He will show up," Wiglaf said, keeping his eyes on Sir Lancelot.

Erica danced close to Wiglaf. Sir Lancelot followed. It was time for action! Wiglaf quickly slipped the mirror out from under his cloak. He held it up to the knight's face.

"Sir!" he cried. "You are not a chicken. You are a noble knight!"

Sir Lancelot looked into the mirror. He cocked his head. He began clucking excitedly. *"Bluck-bluck! Bluck-bluck!"*

"Is it working?" Erica asked. "Is it?"

Before Wiglaf could answer, a voice cried out. "Come back here, hound! Or I'll cut out your liver and roast it!"

Lowly Birth stopped playing. The few remaining party guests raced from the room.

Wiglaf turned. He saw Rufus running toward them carrying a black, fur-trimmed shoe.

Morgana ran after him. She held the mate to the shoe in Rufus's mouth.

"Oh, jester's bells!" Angus moaned as Rufus reached him. "We are doomed!" The dog dropped Morgana's slobber-drenched shoe at his feet.

"How *dare* you gnomes bring a *dog* to my party!" Morgana shrieked. "These are my best shoes!" Then her eyes locked on Sir Lancelot. "Who let my knight out of his cage?" she cried. "You horrid gnomes! I'm turning the lot of you to stone!" She raised her hand.

"You can't turn us to stone!" Erica cried. She whisked off her gnome cap. "We are humans! And we have come to save Sir Lancelot!"

"Not a chance!" Morgana growled. "And who said I couldn't have stone humans in my garden?" She began to chant:

"Noisy boys annoy me so!"

Morgana pointed at Wiglaf. Yellow sparks burst from her fingertips. He was about to be turned to stone!

Chapter 9

"oooo!" Wiglaf cried. He held up Sir Lancelot's mirror to keep Morgana's sparks from hitting him.

Morgana chanted: *"To the garden..."*

Wiglaf squeezed his eyes shut. He did *not* want to turn into a garden statue.

"...you must go!" Morgana chanted.

Wiglaf felt the sparks strike the mirror.

Morgana's voice stopped suddenly.

Silence filled the air.

Wiglaf waited. Had his ears turned to stone? He opened an eye. He peeked over the mirror. He saw Morgana. Her finger still pointed at him. Her hand was strangely still and gray.

And then the truth hit him. Morgana was a stone statue!

"Nice work, Wiggie!" cried Erica.

"But...how?" Wiglaf managed as he struggled to his feet.

"Sir Lancelot's mirror!" Angus exclaimed. "It bounced the sparks back at Morgana!"

Wiglaf saw sparks shimmering in the air in front of him. He stepped back. Did Morgana's power live on? Then...*poof!*

"Tah dah!" Zelnoc cried, spreading his arms wide. "I said I'd be back, Wiglap. And here I am! Whoa, Morgana," he added. "You're looking a little tense, my dear."

"She's turned herself to stone," Angus said.

Zelnoc walked over and knocked on her. "Ha! So she has! Sandstone, I'd say."

"Bluck-bluck-bluck!" clucked Sir Lancelot.

"I see Morgana finally perfected her chicken spell," Zelnoc said. "Shall I undo it?"

"Yes, please," Erica said.

Zelnoc pushed up the sleeves of his wizard's gown. He aimed both pointer fingers at the knight. He began to stomp and chant:

"Boom chicka boom! Boom chicka boom!
Boom chicka-licka-chicka! Boom, boom!
Lip lip sah! Lip lip sah!
Chicken out! Chicken out! Rah rah rah!"

Zelnoc jumped up and landed in a split.

"Bluck-bluck!" cackled Sir Lancelot.

"Rats," said Zelnoc. "Let me try it again." The wizard chanted his spell again. But Sir Lancelot kept on cackling. Zelnoc wiped wizard sweat from his brow.

"Ah ha!" he cried at last. "Morgana didn't change Lance into a chicken. She only made him *think* he's a chicken. This calls for a different spell altogether." Again he began to chant:

"Oh, spell most fowl! Oh, spell that's stricken
Sir Lancelot with brain of chicken!

I wish I may, I wish I might,
Give Lance back a brain of knight!"

As the word *knight* fell from the wizard's lips, Sir Lancelot sprang to his feet. His hands dropped from his armpits. He looked down at his long underwear. He seemed confused.

"Sir Lancelot!" Erica cried, bowing to him.

But Sir Lancelot only frowned. "My sword!" he cried. "My armor! What has become of my knightly trappings?"

Erica beamed. "Here is your glove, sir," she said proudly, handing it to him. "And your helmet. I carried it here all the way from Dragon Slayers' Academy."

Sir Lancelot looked even more confused.

"Here is your mirror, sir," Wiglaf added.

Sir Lancelot gazed into his mirror for quite some time. "I look not well," he said at last. "I must have been in a terrible battle. No doubt I slew many an evil enemy."

He lowered the mirror. "Where am I now?"

"In the palace of Morgana le Fay," Erica answered. "She cast a horrible spell—"

"On you small, helpless children," Sir Lancelot finished for her.

"Uh...not exactly, sir," Erica said.

"Do not thank me, child," Sir Lancelot said.

"Thank *you*?" Erica said.

"You're welcome," Sir Lancelot said. "But it is my duty to help the helpless."

"But, sir—" Erica began.

"Oh, thank me if you must," Sir Lancelot said. "Shower me with violets. Or bow down before me. But remember, I live to save help-less creatures, such as yourselves." The knight set his helmet on his head. "I must find some-one good enough to lend me a suit of armor, a sword, a shield, and a horse," he said. He tucked his mirror under his arm and hurried off in search of knightly trappings.

Zelnoc chuckled. "Gratitude never was Lance's strong point," he said. "I'll take my ring now, Waglaf," he added. He pointed at the green-stoned ring. It floated off Wiglaf's thumb and slid onto the wizard's pinkie.

"I forgot to ask, sir," Wiglaf said. "Does this ring possess magical powers?"

"Only one," Zelnoc said. "It changes lumpen pudding into any dish you wish."

Angus groaned. "Now you tell us!"

"Zelnoc, sir?" Erica said. "Will Morgana stay a stone statue forever?"

"Forever is a long time," the wizard replied.

"Isn't it, though?" said Trog's mother as she strolled into the ballroom. She carried a suitcase. "That's how long I feel I've been away from home. I'm going back to my Trog." She smiled at Wiglaf. "Looks like you've taken care of Morgana after all. Why don't I drop her off in the garden on my way out?" The troll hoisted the statue onto her shoulder. "You've put on some weight, witch," she said. And she carried Morgana out of the ballroom.

When she had gone, Zelnoc whistled loudly.

Rufus dropped what was left of Morgana's shoe. He walked slowly over to the wizard.

"All right, pooch," Zelnoc said. "Are you ready to go back to where you came from?"

"What?" cried Wiglaf. "You mean to say that *you* sent us the dog?"

"Who did you think sent him, Santa Claus?" Zelnoc rolled his eyes. "I said I'd help you, didn't I? All right, dog. Off you go."

The wizard pulled a wand from his sleeve. He began circling it over Rufus's head.

"Stop, wizard!" Erica cried suddenly. "Where are you sending him?"

"Back to my cousin Zerber," Zelnoc said. "He keeps dozens of bloodhounds. Loves to hear them yowl at the moon."

"But this dog has come such a long way with

us, sir," Erica kept on. "I know Angus would like to keep him and be his master."

Angus shook his head. "My mother has allergies. She'd never let me keep a dog."

"Wiglaf then," said Erica.

"I have Daisy to care for," Wiglaf said.

"Zerber will be glad to have you back, pup," Zelnoc said. He raised his wand.

"Wait!" cried Erica.

Rufus thumped his tail.

"I do not care much for dogs," Erica said.

Rufus inched toward Erica. He kept thumping his tail.

Erica sighed. "But maybe—"

Before she could finish, Rufus jumped up onto her. He began licking her face.

Erica did not push him down. Instead, she wrapped her arms around him. "Oh, all right. But no shoe chewing," she warned. "At least none of *my* shoes."

"He's yours, then," Zelnoc told Erica.

"Zerber has so many, he won't miss him. All right. I'm done here. Good-bye, Wiplag."

"I almost forgot," Wiglaf said. "On the way here, we ran into your grandpappy."

Zelnoc whirled around. "The old bat?"

"Yes, sir," Wiglaf said. "He was out front."

Zelnoc smiled. "I'm feeling my powers today," he said. "I'll bet I can free him from his spell." And he hurried from the ballroom.

Light coming in through the ballroom window told Wiglaf that a new day had dawned. The three questers and Rufus made their way out of the palace.

Outside, Wiglaf saw that only the statue of Morgana stood in the palace garden. He guessed that when Morgana had turned to stone, the gnomes had been released from their spells.

Before long, the questers came to the circle of blue-flame torches. And there on a tree stump sat a dejected-looking wizard. Beside him sat a large rat.

"I said I was sorry," Zelnoc muttered.

"At least before I could fly!" the rat squeaked. "Now look at me! People will think I carry the plague! I'm going to report you to the Wizards Commission, Zelnoc! You'll never cast spells in this forest again!"

Zelnoc looked up and saw the questers. He waved. "Farewell, Woglump!" he called. "I'm in a muddle here. But don't worry. I'll figure something out. I always do."

"Farewell, Zelnoc!" Wiglaf called back. "And thank you for your help!"

Just then a knight in shining armor galloped up to them on a black steed. He raised the visor on his helmet.

"It's Sir Lancelot!" Erica exclaimed.

"I am off to Camelot," the knight said. "Good speed on your journey, helpless ones!"

"But we are not—" Erica began.

"Going far?" Sir Lancelot guessed. "That is a good thing. For danger lurks everywhere in the Darkest Forest. Beware! I go now to fight the good fight. To battle evil! Wish me well!"

"Good luck!" Erica called halfheartedly as her knight in shining armor rode away.

"Our quest was a success," Angus reminded Erica as they passed a pair of ogres carrying piles of nettles. "Good won over evil."

"Yes, we saved our knight." Erica sighed.

"Do you wish Sir Lancelot understood what *really* happened?" Wiglaf asked.

Erica nodded.

"I do not blame you," Wiglaf told her. "But think how unhappy he would be if he knew he had been kept in a cage as a chicken."

"You are right, Wiggie," said Erica. "But it is hard that we get no credit for saving him."

"It will be even harder when we get back to DSA," Angus added. "Mordred will be unhappy that we've brought him no reward."

"Be not gloomy," Wiglaf said. "Perchance

something will turn up on our way home. We may have more adventures yet before we reach DSA."

"Yes!" Angus exclaimed. "Who knows what may befall us as we journey on?"

Rufus raised his head and let out a howl. He began sniffing excitedly down the trail.

"Here we come, Ruf!" Erica cried as she and the others ran after him.

"Sniff on, Rufus!" Wiglaf called. For surely the dog was leading them to their next adventure.

~DSA~
YEARBOOK

Goldius est goodius!

The Campus of Dragon Slayers' Academy

~Our Founders~

Sir Herbert Dungeonstone

Sir Ichabod Popquiz

~ Our Philosophy ~

Sir Herbert and Sir Ichabod founded
Dragon Slayers' Academy on a simple
principle still held dear today: Any lad—
no matter how weak, yellow-bellied, lazy,
pigeon-toed, smelly, or unwilling—can be
transformed into a fearless dragon slayer
who goes for the gold. After four years
at DSA, lads will finally be of some
worth to their parents, as well as a
source of great wealth to this distin-
guished academy.* ** ***

* Please note that Dragon Slayers' Academy is a strictly-for-profit
institution.

** Dragon Slayers' Academy reserves the right to keep some of the gold
and treasure that any student recovers from a dragon's lair.

*** The exact amount of treasure given to a student's family is deter-
mined solely by our esteemed headmaster, Mordred. The amount shall be
no less than 1/500th of the treasure and no greater than 1/499th.

Mordred de Marvelous

Mordred graduated from Dragon Bludgeon High, second in his class. The other student, Lionel Flyzwattar, went on to become headmaster of Dragon Stabbers' Prep. Mordred spent years as part-time, semi-substitute student teacher at Dragon Whackers' Alternative School, all the while pursuing his passion for mud wrestling. Inspired by how filthy rich Flyzwattar had become by running a school, Mordred founded Dragon Slayers' Academy in CMLXXIV, and has served as headmaster ever since.

⚜

Known to the Boys as: Mordred de Miser
Dream: Piles and piles of dragon gold
Reality: Yet to see a single gold coin
Best-Kept Secret: Mud wrestled under the name
Macho-Man Mordie
Plans for the Future: Will retire to the Bahamas ... as
soon as he gets his hands on a hoard

Lady Lobelia

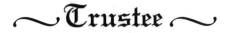

Lobelia de Marvelous is Mordred's sister and a graduate of the exclusive If-You-Can-Read-This-You-Can-Design-Clothes Fashion School. Lobelia has offered fashion advice to the likes of King Felix the Husky and Eric the Terrible Dresser. In CMLXXIX, Lobelia married the oldest living knight, Sir Jeffrey Scabpicker III. That's when she gained the title of Lady Lobelia, but—alas!—only a very small fortune, which she wiped out in a single wild shopping spree. Lady Lobelia has graced Dragon Slayers' Academy with many visits, and can be heard around campus saying, "Just because I live in the Middle Ages doesn't mean I have to look middle-aged."

⚜

Known to the Boys as: Lady Lo Lo
Dream: Frightfully fashionable
Reality: Frightful
Best-Kept Secret: Shops at Dark-Age Discount Dress Dungeon
Plans for the Future: New uniforms for the boys with mesh tights and lace tunics

Sir Mort du Mort

Sir Mort is our well-loved professor of Dragon Slaying for Beginners as well as Intermediate and Advanced Dragon Slaying. Sir Mort says that, in his youth, he was known as the Scourge of Dragons. (We're not sure what it means, but it sounds scary.) His last encounter was with the most dangerous dragon of them all: Knight-shredder. Early in the battle, Sir Mort took a nasty blow to his helmet and has never been the same since.

❦

Known to the Boys as: The Old Geezer
Dream: Outstanding Dragon Slayer
Reality: Just plain out of it
Best-Kept Secret: He can't remember
Plans for the Future: Taking a little nap

Coach Wendell Plungett

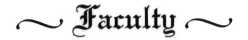

Coach Plungett spent many years questing in the Dark Forest before joining the Athletic Department at DSA. When at last he strode out of the forest, leaving his dragon-slaying days behind him, Coach Plungett was the most muscle-bulging, physically fit, manliest man to be found anywhere north of Nowhere Swamp. "I am what you call a hunk," the coach admits. At DSA, Plungett wears a number of hats—or, helmets. Besides PE Teacher, he is Slaying Coach, Square-Dance Director, Pep-Squad Sponsor, and Privy Inspector. He hopes to meet a damsel—she needn't be in distress—with whom he can share his love of heavy metal music and long dinners by candlelight.

❦

Known to the Boys as: Coach
Dream: Tough as nails
Reality: Sleeps with a stuffed dragon named Foofoo
Best-Kept Secret: Just pull his hair
Plans for the Future: Finding his lost lady love

Brother Dave

Brother Dave is the DSA librarian. He belongs to the Little Brothers of the Peanut Brittle, an order known for doing impossibly good deeds and cooking up endless batches of sweet peanut candy. How exactly did Brother Dave wind up at Dragon Slayers' Academy? After a batch of his extra-crunchy peanut brittle left three children from Toenail toothless, Brother Dave vowed to do a truly impossible good deed. Thus did he offer to be librarian at a school world-famous for considering reading and writing a complete and utter waste of time. Brother Dave hopes to change all that.

❧

Known to the Boys as: Bro Dave
Dream: Boys reading in the libary
Reality: Boys sleeping in the library
Best-Kept Secret: Uses Cliff's Notes
Plans for the Future: Copying out all the lyrics to "Found a Peanut" for the boys

Professor Prissius Pluck

Professor Pluck graduated from Peter Piper Picked a Peck of Pickled Peppers Prep, and went on to become a professor of Science at Dragon Slayers' Academy. His specialty is the Multiple Choice Pop Test. The boys who take Dragon Science, Professor Pluck's popular class,

a) are amazed at the great quantities of saliva Professor P. can project

b) try never to sit in the front row

c) beg Headmaster Mordred to transfer them to another class

d) all of the above

❖

Known to the Boys as: Old Spit Face

Dream: Proper pronunciation of *p*'s

Reality: Let us spray

Best-Kept Secret: Has never seen a pippi-hippo-pappa-peepus up close

Plans for the Future: Is working on a cure for chapped lips

Frypot

How Frypot came to be the cook at DSA is something of a mystery. Rumors abound. Some say that when Mordred bought the broken-down castle for his school, Frypot was already in the kitchen and he simply stayed on. Others say that Lady Lobelia hired Frypot because he was so speedy at washing dishes. Still others say Frypot knows many a dark secret that keeps him from losing his job. But no one ever, *ever* says that Frypot was hired because of his excellent cooking skills.

⚜

Known to the Boys as: Who needs a nickname with a real name like Frypot?
Dream: Cleaner kitchen
Reality: Kitchen cleaner
Best-Kept Secret: Takes long bubble baths in the moat
Plans for the Future: Has signed up for a beginning cooking class

Yorick

Yorick is Chief Scout at DSA. His knack for masquerading as almost anything comes from his years with the Merry Minstrels and Dancing Damsels Players, where he won an award for his role as the Glass Slipper in "Cinderella". However, when he was passed over for the part of Mama Bear in "Goldilocks", Yorick decided to seek a new way of life. He snuck off in the night and, by dawn, still dressed in the bear suit,
found himself walking up Huntsmans Path. Mordred spied him from a castle window, recognized his talent for disguise, and hired him as Chief Scout on the spot.

❖

Known to the Boys as: Who's that?
Dream: Master of Disguise
Reality: Mordred's Errand Boy
Best-Kept Secret: Likes dressing up as King Ken
Plans for the Future: To lose the bunny suit

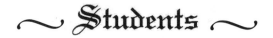

Wiglaf of Pinwick

Wiglaf, our newest lad, hails from a hovel outside the village of Pinwick, which makes Toenail look like a thriving metropolis. Being one of thirteen children, Wiglaf had a taste of dorm life before coming to DSA and he fit right in. He started the year off with a bang when he took a stab at Coach Plungett's brown pageboy wig. Way to go, Wiggie! We hope to see more of this lad's wacky humor in the years to come.

❧

Dream: Bold Dragon-Slaying Hero
Reality: Still hangs on to a "security" rag
Extracurricular Activities: Animal-Lovers Club, President; No More Eel for Lunch Club, President; Frypot's Scrub Team, Brush Wielder; Pig Appreciation Club, Founder
Favorite Subject: Library
Oft-Heard Saying: *"Ello-hay, Aisy-day!"*
Plans for the Future: To go for the gold!